P9-DEE-332

THAT'S EXACTLY THE WAY IT WASN'T

by James Stevenson

Greenwillow Books, New York

Hammond Public Library
Hammond, Ind.

*Watercolor paints and
a black pen were used
for the full-color art.
The text type is
ITC Clearface.*

*Copyright © 1991
by James Stevenson
All rights reserved.
No part of this book
may be reproduced or
utilized in any form
or by any means,
electronic or mechanical,
including photocopying,
recording, or by any
information storage
and retrieval system,
without permission in
writing from the Publisher,
Greenwillow Books,
a division of William
Morrow & Company, Inc.,
105 Madison Avenue,
New York, NY 10016.
Printed in Hong Kong
by South China Printing
Company (1988) Ltd.
First Edition
10 9 8 7 6 5 4 3 2 1*

*Library of Congress
Cataloging-in-Publication Data*

*Stevenson, James (date)
That's exactly the way it wasn't/
by James Stevenson.
p.   cm.
Summary:
Grandpa and Wainey
tell Mary Ann and Louie
different versions of
the same story.
ISBN 0-688-09868-1.
ISBN 0-688-09869-X (lib. bdg.)
[1. Grandfathers—Fiction.
2. Brothers and sisters—Fiction.
3. Humorous stories.]
I. Title.
PZ7.S84748Ti   1991
[E]—dc20
90-30749   CIP   AC*

"Hello, Mary Ann! Hello, Louie!" called Grandpa.
"Enjoying a bit of fresh air on this splendid day?"
"No, Grandpa," said Louie. "Our parents told us to take
a long walk, because Mary Ann was arguing all the time."
"No, I wasn't," said Mary Ann. "Louie was."
"See?" said Louie. "She's doing it again."

"Isn't that strange?" said Grandpa. "My brother Wainey had the same problem."

"That's not the way I remember it," said Grandpa.
"How *do* you remember it?" asked Louie.

"Well, when Wainey and I were young, we lived in a white house on Elm Street," said Grandpa....

"Excuse me," said Uncle Wainey.
"A red house on Maple Avenue."

"With our yellow cat, Hilda," said Grandpa.

"I believe you mean our black dog, Oliver," said Uncle Wainey.

"In those days," said Grandpa, "Wainey always howled if he didn't get his own way."

"Not exactly," said Uncle Wainey. "I never got my own way. You were always bossing me around."

"One day our parents got fed up with us," said Grandpa.

"We walked for miles and miles,"
said Grandpa.
"Didn't you get tired?" said Mary Ann.
"Yes," said Grandpa. "Especially when
Wainey made me carry him."

"Finally, I just couldn't go any farther."

"Because," said Grandpa, "that's when the armadillo came along.

The armadillo gave us shelter until the landslide ended.

Then he curled up...."

"I followed the 'WAHs,'" said Grandpa.

"I hushed hundreds of ducks and geese....

At last I had it down to one 'WAH'...but it wasn't Wainey.

It was just a parrot imitating the ducks and geese."

"During the landslide, your grandpa kept telling the armadillo what to do," said Uncle Wainey.

"As soon as the landslide ended, the armadillo and I ran away,"
  Uncle Wainey continued.

"When the armadillo went home, I looked for your grandpa....
I found him arguing with a parrot."

"It seemed like my big chance with Wainey," said Grandpa.

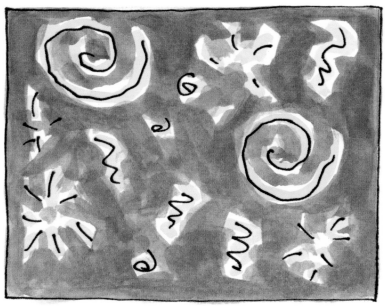

"It was pretty dark for a while."

"It was cold and dark."

"Just a moment," said Uncle Wainey. "To the best of my memory, that was not a *cave*."

"What was it?" asked Mary Ann.

"It was an iguana's mouth," said Uncle Wainey.
"I believe you're right," said Grandpa, "now that I think of it....

Wainey made a terrible fuss.
Finally, the iguana couldn't stand it
another minute."

"The speech went on and on until...

the iguana got so bored he began to yawn. We jumped out…

We fell through a lot of smoke and landed on something hot and bubbly.

There was a lot of shaking...."

"Because it was about to erupt!" said Grandpa.

"And it did," said Uncle Wainey.

"We sailed through the air," said Grandpa, "and...

arrived home just in time for supper."

Hammond Public Library
Hammond, Ind.

3 1161 00460 6003